D2

Secret Tre

Collect all the Charmseekers –

The Queen's Bracelet
The Silver Pool
The Dragon's Revenge
A Tale of Two Sisters
The Fragile Force
The Stolen Goblet
The Magic Crystals
Secret Treasure

from October 2011
Star Island
Moonlight and Mermaids

from 2012
The Mirror of Deception
Zorgan and the Gorsemen
The Last Portal

www.charmseekers.co.uk

Secret Treasure

Georgie Adams

Illustrated by Gwen Millward

Orion
Children's Books

First published in Great Britain in 2009
by Orion Children's Books
Reissued 2011 by Orion Children's Books
a division of the Orion Publishing Group Ltd
Orion House
5 Upper St Martin's Lane
London WC2H 9EA
An Hachette UK Company

1 3 5 7 9 8 6 4 2

A catalogue record for this book is
available from the British Library.

ISBN: 978 1 4440 0296 6

Printed and bound in the UK by
CPI Mackays, Chatham ME5 8TD

www.orionbooks.co.uk
www.charmseekers.co.uk

For Rosemary Sandberg, with love

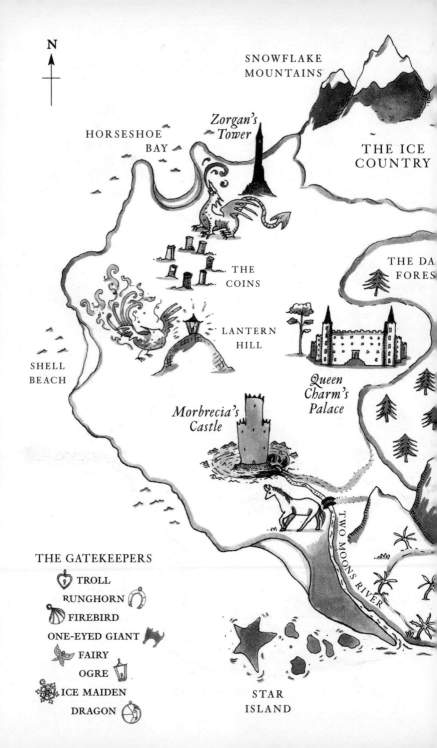

N

SNOWFLAKE
MOUNTAINS

*Zorgan's
Tower*

HORSESHOE
BAY

THE ICE
COUNTRY

THE DA
FORES

THE
COINS

SHELL
BEACH

LANTERN
HILL

*Queen
Charm's
Palace*

*Morbrecia's
Castle*

TWO MOONS RIVER

THE GATEKEEPERS

TROLL
RUNGHORN
FIREBIRD
ONE-EYED GIANT
FAIRY
OGRE
ICE MAIDEN
DRAGON

STAR
ISLAND

The Thirteen Charms of Karisma

When Charm became queen of Karisma, the wise and beautiful Silversmith made her a precious gift. It was a bracelet. On it were fastened thirteen silver amulets, which the Silversmith called 'charms', in honour of the new queen.

It was part of Karisma law. Whenever there was a new ruler the Silversmith made a special gift, to help them care for the world they had inherited. And this time it was a bracelet. She told Queen Charm it was magical because the charms held the power to control the forces of nature and keep everything in balance. She must take the greatest care of them. As long as she, and she alone, had possession of the charms all would be well.

And so it was, until the bracelet was stolen by a spider, and fell into the hands of Zorgan, the magician. Then there was chaos!

1

One

"Who is Jason Flook?" asked Lois Brown, over supper one evening. Lois was Sesame's gran, but everyone called her Lossy. She tried to conceal a smile, as she spoke to her granddaughter.

"G-r-a-n," Sesame groaned. "Jason Flook is only *the* most gorgeous film star ever! You must have heard of him. He was the coolest pirate captain in *Treasure Seekers* and now he's making this brill new film—"

Sesame stopped when she saw Lossy exchange amused glances with her dad, Nic. "Oh, very funny, Gran. I might have known you were teasing!"

"Sorry," said Lossy. "Yes, of course I know who Jason Flook is. Just think! You might meet him tomorrow."

"Ooo, Dad!" said Sesame, hardly able to breathe she was so excited. "Do you think I will?"

"I'll try and fix it," said Nic. "On one condition. Promise me you won't faint. I don't want you to ruin a good picture!"

They had been talking about Star Productions' new action-packed adventure, *Tomb Robbers*. It was being filmed on location near an ancient burial site, and Nic had been booked for a photo shoot. The job fell during half-term, so he'd arranged for Sesame and her friends to come too.

After supper, Sesame raced upstairs to her room and chatted to Maddy, Gemma and Liz online:

seekerSes@zoom.com says:
Hi, everyone! Ready to meet You Know Who? Wot R U wearing? I can't decide!

MadWebbgirl@mailwizard.net says:
Yeah. We must look super glam for J.F. Ha, ha! Eeek! I've dropped a fake nail on the carpet.

funkygemG@helloo.com says:
Your dad's super-cool, Ses. Can't beleeeve I'm going on a film set. Celebs here we come! I'm soooo excited.

charmLizzy@chat2U.com says:
Me too. Won't sleep a wink tonight.

What time are we meeting at your house, Ses?

seekerSes@zoom.com says:
Come at 9. Dad says be on time (MadWebbgirl!)

See you all 2moz. Mwah Mwah x

Next morning, everyone arrived at Sesame's house on time – even Maddy! The girls piled into Nic's car, chatting excitedly. It took over an hour to drive to the location – a wild sweeping moor, famous for its ancient standing stones. On the way, the girls talked non-stop about their favourite pop stars, music, TV and film celebs, clothes, make-up and hair.

"Phew!" said Nic, when they eventually arrived. "It's amazing what you girls find to talk about!"

An attractive young woman holding a clipboard waved to them across the car park and came over. She had long black hair and was wearing a bright yellow top, skinny jeans and funky trainers.

"Hi!" she greeted them. "I'm Samira. Director's Assistant."

After introductions
Samira said:

"I'll show the girls around,
Nic. We'll meet up after the photo
shoot. Okay?"

"Great," said Nic. "Have fun."

Sesame, Maddy, Gemma and Liz followed
Samira through a jumble of trucks, trailers,
catering vans, cameras, cables and lighting
equipment. There were film crew
and technicians everywhere;
a man from the wardrobe
department carrying an armful
of costumes; a hair stylist spraying
a wig; noisy carpenters building scenery

and actors studying their scripts
and rehearsing their lines. There
was so much to take in all at once!
Sesame couldn't resist asking the one
question they'd all been longing to know
the answer to:

"Where's Jason Flook?"

Before Samira had time to reply, some riggers
came along manoeuvring a golden
dragon. The huge prop was on a trolley
and men were hauling it with ropes.

"Mind your backs!" shouted one.

Samira jumped out of the way, but
Sesame stepped backwards and tripped
over a trailing rope . . .

"Whooooops!" she cried.

"Steady there," said a gentle voice.

Sesame looked up to see a gorgeous young man with fair hair, deep blue eyes and a boyish face smiling down at her. It was Jason Flook!

"Here," said Jason, offering Sesame his hand. "Let me help you."

"Er, th-thanks," said Sesame, blushing red as a radish.

Maddy, Gemma and Liz stood awestruck, jaws dropping, eyes open wide. Samira grinned at Sesame.

"You were saying?" she said.

The next few minutes whizzed by. Jason chatted and joked with the girls and signed their autograph books, until his mobile rang.

8

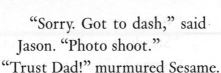

"Sorry. Got to dash," said Jason. "Photo shoot."

"Trust Dad!" murmured Sesame.

"Samira, could you show me the way?" said Jason.

"Of course," she said. "Back in five, girls!"

She left Sesame, Maddy, Gemma and Liz to look around the burial chamber set. There was a sarcophagus, ornately carved and flanked by fierce-looking monsters. All around it were scattered gold coins and behind it stood the dragon.

"I know this coffin thing is fake," said Maddy, daring to touch the sarcophagus. "But it looks so real."

Liz gave a little shiver.

"Mm," she said. "Spooky!"

"It's fascinating—" began Gemma, but catching sight of Sesame, she stopped. Sesame was swaying slightly and looked as if she might faint. "Are you okay?"

"My head's spinning," said Sesame. "Everything's going round and round." She felt a gentle breeze on her cheeks, then suddenly she was tumbling head-over-heels and falling into a magical mist. "Maddy! Gemma! Liz!" she heard herself cry, only her voice seemed a million miles away. Next thing she knew, the others were flying with her through a cascade of silvery stars. They were on their way to Karisma!

Two

When Dina returned from the Ice Country, Zorgan had ranted and raged at her. He'd sent the pixie on a mission to snatch Sesame's locket, and she'd failed – just like Nix. As a punishment he ordered Dina to sit on the roof of his tower and repeat a million times: "I must not fail."

That was a mede* ago, and she was *still* chanting!

Now the magician paced the floor of his Star Room, vengeful thoughts swirling inside his head.

"I must have Sesame's locket!" he told Vanda, his pet bandrall.** The bird-like creature had perched on his shoulder and Zorgan was stroking her scraggy neck. "If I had hold of Sesame's locket, I could put her under a spell. Then she'd be compelled to bring ME all the charms. Hm! I must think of a way to get it . . ."

* *
* **Mede** – month
** **Bandrall** – rare flying mammal, native to Karisma

11

Zorgan considered how best to achieve this aim without anyone suspecting him. He had once tried (unsuccessfully) to turn his old enemy, the Silversmith, against Sesame Brown.

"Pah!" he snorted, remembering the Silversmith's angry response. "I might have known she'd defend her Seeker to the end. But maybe I could persuade Queen Charm instead? If *she* suspected Sesame of stealing her charms, she'd order Sesame's arrest. And if Sesame were held prisoner in the palace, I'd have a chance to snatch her locket. Well, not me. I'd transform Morbrecia into a spider again, so she could steal it! It worked with Charm's bracelet. I'm sure Morbrecia would fall in with my plans. But first I must deal with Charm . . ."

Zorgan hurried down a spiral staircase, one hundred and ninety five twisty steps, to his library. His vast collection of books on magic had once been ruined by drakons* – a spiteful act of revenge by Agapogo, he recalled, and all because he'd invoked the dragon to drain the Silver Pool. It had taken him time (and a considerable number of spells!) to restore his beautiful room full of books.

* *
* **Drakon** – a large, fire-breathing insect

Zorgan looked at the thousands of volumes on the shelves and it gave him great pleasure. Every one of the leather-bound books had been dusted by Nix, which had been *her* punishment for failing to steal Sesame's locket! He scanned the shelves, until one particular title caught his attention:

RARE CHANTS AND INCANTATIONS
* REVISED EDITION *
New and improved spells for every occasion

he read on the cover. He opened it, flicked through the pages till he came to page one hundred and fifty nine.

13

SEEDS OF DOUBT
A powerful spell, which sows seeds of doubt or suspicious thoughts in the mind of another. The unsuspecting recipient of these

159

intoxicating flowers will experience a complete change of mind about someone or something, within a few grickles * of smelling their scent.

160

"Perfect!" he said. "I'll try it at once!"

After adding names and a few details to the spell, Zorgan intoned these words over a handful of seeds:

> Seeds of doubt, grow into flowers,
> A sweet bouquet of magic powers.
> Fragrant scent, swell every bloom,
> Fill Charm's head with thoughts of gloom!
> Let doubts, like shadows, cross her mind;
> Her trust in Sesame has been blind.
> Let it be Charm's belief;
> The girl is nothing but a thief!

* *

Grickle – about the same time as a second in our world

14

The last word had barely left the magician's lips, when the seeds burst into a magnificent bouquet of dark purple flowers.

"Spallah!"* exclaimed Zorgan, clapping his hands. "Now for a suitable time to send them to Charm. I don't want to arouse her suspicions."

Glancing at his calendar he realised that this was the mede of Elar, when the queen celebrated her birthday. As luck would have it, today was the day! Quickly Zorgan conjured a birthday card, wrote a greeting then sent it and the flowers to the palace.

* *

* Spallah – excellent! A triumphant expression

Three

Sesame landed with a bump beside a wall, which had a row of shiny spikes along the top. At least that's what she thought they were, until they twitched. Seconds later, Maddy, Gemma and Liz landed nearby.

Thump, thump, thump!

"What the—?" began Maddy, picking herself up and peering at the pinkish-silvery scales, glinting in the early morning sun.

"It's a t-t-tail," said Sesame. "I saw it move."

"Gross!" said Gemma.

Liz gulped and pointed. "Look!"

The girls looked where she was pointing, along the length of the tail, which was attached to an

16

enormous body. Two leathery wings were folded across the back and at the end of a very long neck, there was the head of – a dragon! The dragon was snoring loudly and, with each snuffling snort, he blew a blast of hot air in their direction. To everyone's horror, he suddenly opened one eye and seemed very surprised to see them.

"Hurrumph! Ahem! Um, well now," he began, in a I-wasn't-really-asleep sort of way. "Where did *you* come from?"

Sesame hid a smile. It was obvious the dragon was embarrassed to have been caught snoozing. She introduced everyone and told him they were from a world a long way away.

"Ahhhhh!"

said the dragon, hissing steam from his nostrils like a pressure cooker. "You're Charmseekers! Fairday.*
Welcome to Karisma! I'm Pogo, Gatekeeper Eight. You're the first visitors to come through my gate. I've never met anyone from the Outworld**
before."

They were standing outside Pogo's cave and Gemma noticed a roll of parchment on the ground.

* *
* Fairday – a typical Karisman friendly greeting
** Outworld – the name Karismans call our world

17

"What's that?" she asked.

Pogo seemed delighted to show it to her.

"My family tree!" he said. "It's a bit scorched, I'm afraid. Do you know, I can trace my family back to Agapogo."

"Cool!" said Sesame. She remembered the time she and Maddy had been told the Legend of the Silver Pool.★ "Agapogo was the poor dragon who drowned in silver, wasn't she?"

★ ★

★ **The Legend of the Silver Pool** – do you remember the story? You'll find it in *Book Two: The Silver Pool*

18

"Yes," said Pogo. "I'm very proud of my ancestor.
I wish I knew more about her. There was a time
when we dragons—"

Sesame was afraid he would keep them talking
about dragons all day, so she quickly changed
the subject.

"We've come to look for the charms
that are still lost," she said.

"Oh, the magical charms!" said Pogo wistfully.
"Which ones?"

"The key, dolphin, star, moon, cloverleaf and
coin," replied Sesame.

"Hm, the silver coin . . ." said Pogo dreamily.
He yawned. "There's a ring of standing stones
called The Coins. You might start looking
there?" He yawned again and his eyelids
drooped.

Sesame had a feeling they *might* find the coin
there. Anyway it was worth a try.

"How will we find them?" she asked.

"Map," said Pogo sleepily. He produced
a crumpled map from under his wing and
gave it to Sesame. "Be sure to be back by the
Seventh Shadow—"

The last word trailed away.

"What does *that* mean?" asked Maddy.

But Pogo had fallen asleep. The Charmseekers
would have to work it out for themselves!

Sesame spread out the map, so they could all see
where they were. Maddy spotted a circle of dots.
"I reckon they must be the standing stones," she
said.

"Oh, look," said Liz, pointing to four specks of
light.

"That's us!" said Sesame. "They track our
position. I had a map like this, the first time I came
to Karisma."

"Wicked!" said Gemma.

And they set off to look for The Coins.

On the way, they noticed a tall, dark tower in the
distance.

"Ooo!" said Maddy. "I think that's Zorgan's
tower. Ses, remember what the Snow Bear told us,
when he helped us in the Ice Country?"

"Yes," said Sesame. "If you're right, it's where Zorgan threw the charms away!"

"What *are* you talking about?" asked Gemma.

"Come on, tell us," said Liz.

So Sesame and Maddy told them what they'd found out about Zorgan, the last time they came to Karisma. By the time they'd finished, they had come to a grassy mound swathed in morning mist. They could just make out the blurred outline of a standing stone, rising eerily from the ground, and when they went to investigate they found the lower part of the stone had some carvings, partly covered by moss. Liz scraped the moss away and discovered a number with some strange words carved below it.

At first none of them could make any sense of it, but Sesame loved puzzles and cracking codes and soon saw a way to solve this one.

21

IN A CIRCLE,
SEVEN STONES,
GUARDIANS OF OLD
DRAGON BONES.
CURSED TREASURE
LIES BELOW,
WHERE ONLY
FOOLISH FOLK
DARE GO!

Standing Stone Message:
Can you see what Sesame read in the mirror?

"Has anyone got a mirror?" she said. "I think this is mirror-writing!"

"Here," Maddy said. "Have mine."

Sesame wrote the words in her autograph book, near Jason Flook's signature. Seeing his name suddenly took her back to the set of *Tomb Robbers*. It all seemed so far away now, but the film location had been near an ancient burial mound. Weird! Meanwhile, Gemma couldn't contain her excitement.

"Wow! Treasure!" she cried. "I bet there's an entrance somewhere—"

She stopped. Sesame was frowning and pointing to the words on the standing stone.

"Gemma, don't be crazy. It says *cursed* treasure! It's a warning. Anyway, we must find another charm. The coin might be here."

"Oh, don't be such a spoilsport," said Gemma. "We're standing on buried treasure! Come on. We can look for the charm later."

"No way!" said Sesame. "You don't understand. Horrible things are happening in Karisma because Zorgan threw the charms away. And they'll get worse until the charms are found. We haven't got time to look for stupid treasure and mess about with dragon bones!"

Maddy nodded. "I agree," she said. "I'm with you, Ses."

"Oh, surprise, surprise," said Gemma, goggling her eyes. "How about you, Liz? Are you coming?"

23

Liz's glasses had steamed up and she took them off to give them a wipe. She hated arguments! While Sesame and Gemma had been squabbling, she'd been thinking about the inscription on the stone. It *was* intriguing . . .

"Well?" demanded Gemma.

"Okay," said Liz. "I'll come."

Four

Charm was up bright and early on the morning of her birthday. After breakfast, she went to the window and looked out. Despite all the trouble in Karisma, the sun was shining and she was looking forward to seeing her friends later, to celebrate. There was a tap on the door and her maid Ozina came in.

"Good morning, Your Majesty," she said. "Happy Birthday! You've got lots of cards this morning. And these flowers have just arrived."

She presented Charm with a bouquet of dark purple blooms.

"Oh, how beautiful!" said Charm. "I wonder who sent them?" She saw the card and read:

To Her Majesty,
Happy Birthday!
from a well-wisher
x x

"Curious," said Charm. "I don't recognise the handwriting." Then somehow she couldn't resist burying her nose in the petals. "Mm! They have a lovely smell."

And she inhaled their intoxicating scent.

As Ozina left the room, she bumped into Dork, who was on guard duty in the corridor.

"I think Her Maj has got a secret admirer!" she told him.

It took no time at all for the spell to work. As Charm opened her birthday cards, her head began to ache and she found herself thinking about Sesame. And the more her head ached, the more she thought about Sesame, until she thought she had a headache because Sesame was stealing her charms! Dreadful thoughts about the Silversmith's special Charmseeker buzzed like wasps in her head.

Charm twisted a strand of hair round her finger. She was having serious doubts about the judgement of her dearest friend. Could the Silversmith, who she trusted completely, have been wrong about Sesame? Charm had believed her when she'd said Sesame had a gift to seek and find her charms. Perhaps Sesame had a gift for keeping them too! Where *was* her silver bracelet? Where *were* the charms Sesame had found? In the Outworld, that's where! How could the Silversmith be so sure her Seeker would bring them back?

Charm crossed the room and flung the door open.

"Organise a search party," she ordered Dork. "Next time Sesame Brown comes to Karisma, arrest her. My sister was right. The girl is a thief!"

Dork saluted smartly.

"Yes, Your Majesty," he said. "Happy Birthday!"

Dork was pleased to be back in the queen's good books, although he couldn't think how it had come about. When he'd tried to arrest Sesame near Butterfly Bay, Charm said he'd made a terrible mistake. Well, he thought, orders are orders. It's not for me to question Her Maj. My duty is to obey and *this* time I won't let Sesame get away.

Later that morning Dork and his soldiers were passing Morbrecia's castle. He spotted Morbrecia high on the battlements, peering through a small telescope.

The princess saw him too.

"What are you doing here?" she yelled. "I suppose my sister sent you to spy on me again? Well, tell her she won't be getting a birthday present from me!"

"N-n-no, Your Highness," stuttered Dork, craning his neck to speak to her. He was always a little afraid of the hot-tempered princess. "I have orders to arrest Sesame Brown."

"Really?" said Morbrecia. This was surprising news. "What's changed her mind?"

"Couldn't say," said Dork. "But Her Majesty says you were right to suspect Sesame. We're keeping a sharp look out for her return. Er, the view from your battlements must be excellent, Your Royal Highness. W-w-would you be k-k-kind enough to have a quick look for her?"

"Very well," snapped Morbrecia. It was precisely what she'd been doing anyway, but she didn't tell Dork. If Sesame *was* on the trail of another charm and happened to find one, she wanted to be there to grab it. She put the spyglass to her eye and saw a strange, dark cloud hovering over Charm's palace.

29

How odd, she thought. A purple cloud in a clear blue sky! But she thought no more of it because, just then, four moving figures caught her attention. They were walking near an ancient circle of standing stones . . .

"Vixee!"* she cried, punching the air. "The Charmseekers are back!"

* *

* **Vixee** – a gleeful, triumphant expression meaning 'great' or 'wicked'

Five

"I wonder why they're called The Coins?" said Maddy. "They don't *look* like coins."

"Haven't a clue," said Sesame, kicking at a tuft of grass. She was upset about quarrelling with Gemma, but she knew she was right. We're Charmseekers, she said to herself. We're here to look for the charms!

The early morning mist had cleared, revealing more standing stones – each with a number carved on the side. Sesame and Maddy had searched around six stones and were now standing by the last one – stone number seven.

"This one's taller than the rest," observed Maddy.

She thought no more of it because suddenly they both heard a startled cry. A few minutes later, Liz came running towards them, waving her arms.

"Come quickly!" she yelled. "It's Gemma. She needs our help!"

Sesame and Maddy didn't hesitate, they ran like the wind after Liz. She led them to a patch of ground that had given way.

"Gemma's fallen down there," she panted. "I called and called but there was no answer. What if she's—"

Sesame was already on her hands and knees, tearing at weeds and roots; the others helped her, until they'd cleared an opening. Liz feared the worse as they peered into the gloomy darkness of a deep shaft, which had foot and handholds in one wall.

"I'll climb down," said Sesame.

"Be careful!" said Maddy. "I'm coming with you."

"Me too," said Liz, trying to be brave. But when they reached the bottom, there was no sight or sound of Gemma. She had completely disappeared.

"What about the map, Ses?" suggested Maddy. "Gemma *might* show up on it."

"Brill!" said Sesame. "Why didn't I think of that?"

Hastily, she unfolded the map. Sure enough, there was a solitary speck of light, weaving its way along a twisty passage.

"Oh, no!" wailed Liz. "Gemma's gone right inside. I'm scared. I can't go in there."

She began to cry, so Maddy tried to comfort her.

"It's okay," she said. "You stay here. I'll go with Ses. Your light on the map will help us find our way back."

"Thanks," said Liz.

They gave each other their secret Charmseekers hand sign for luck, before they parted.

33

Sesame and Maddy started along a narrow tunnel, following Gemma's illuminated speck on the map. All around them was a greenish half-light and the dreadful smell of rotten eggs.

"Pooo!" exclaimed Maddy, grabbing a hanky from her pocket and holding it over her nose.

Sesame coughed and spluttered.

"Yeah. Worse than gribblers,"* she said. "And they were bad enough!"

* * *
* *

* *
* **Gribbler** – extremely unpleasant goblin-like creature with yellow teeth and bad breath

Meanwhile Gemma was making her way towards a chamber at the centre of the burial mound. She seemed oblivious to the foul aroma filling the air. All she could hear were eerie voices inside her head, urging her on:

I am Smoulder, I am Fume,
Come into our ancient tomb!
Fortune hunter, have no fear,
The gold you seek is waiting here.

Gemma had fallen under the curse of two dragon spirits! She was like a sleepwalker, unaware of her surroundings or the dangers that lay ahead. But when she entered the burial chamber . . . it was as if a switch had been snapped on. Nothing could have prepared her for the sight that met her eyes. A glittering, gleaming hoard of gold filled the room – golden rings, goblets, coins, dishes, jewelled crowns and priceless treasures were piled high, from floor to ceiling. Her jaw dropped and her eyes sparkled with delight.

"Wicked!" she said.

And she reached for a big, shiny bracelet . .

Her fingers had barely touched the bangle, when there s a blinding flash of green light. Two terrifying dragon spectres rose from the treasure, their scales glowing in the gloom, their stinking breath engulfing her. Gemma jumped back and screamed, and once again their ghostly voices filled her head:

Six

Far away on Mount Fortuna, the Silversmith was getting ready to go to the palace. She had received an invitation from Queen Charm, to attend her birthday celebrations that evening.

Her Majesty, Queen Charm of Karisma, requests the pleasure of your company at a party to celebrate The Queen's Birthday at Moonrise on the Eighth day of Elar.

·•● The Palace ●•·

"I wish I could give Charm her bracelet," the Silversmith told a little bird, which had perched on her windowsill. "That would be the *best* birthday present!"

She sighed as she looked at the thirteen magic candles. Six remained burning brightly, waiting for their charms to be found. "I must be patient. My special Seeker has seven magical charms in her safekeeping and I have no doubt she'll find the others too, in time."

The Silversmith wandered into her garden to pick some poppies for the queen.

"If I can't give Charm her bracelet, I shall take her these instead." She tied them with a pretty ribbon. "There – flowers fit for a queen!" But as she said it, a sharp pain gripped her temples, like a vice.

"Hushish!"* she exclaimed. "Something is wrong."

The Silversmith hurried inside, her heart pounding.

"*Memora compozay tribulato!*" she said. It was an old saying, passed on through generations of Silversmiths. "Remember to keep calm in difficulties!"

She closed her eyes and an image of a swirling purple cloud swam into view. It was hovering right over the palace! Was it a bad omen? Was Charm ill? Perhaps she was in danger!

* *
*Hushish – a word used to express dismay

Suddenly the vision of Sesame broke through the haze, and now the Silversmith sensed her *Seeker* was in danger. Sesame was in Karisma, in a dark place associated with long-dead dragons!

The image wavered. She pressed her fingertips to her temples, the better to concentrate.

"Ah!" she sighed. "Sesame is wearing her locket. Good. And I see a silvery aura round her. If she *is* threatened by dragon ghosts, the aura will shield her."

Seven

"Aaaaaah!"

Sesame and Maddy froze when they heard Gemma's chilling scream. It pierced the silence of the tomb and sent shivers down their spines.

"Oh, Ses," Maddy whispered, her voice quivering. "Gemma's in trouble. I wonder what's happened?"

Sesame's stomach churned, her legs felt like jelly and she thought she was going to be sick. But as she stood there with Maddy, she felt her necklace tingle; her locket was warm on her skin and, quite unexpectedly, a surge of courage flowed through her. Sesame couldn't explain it, but she just *knew* she could face whatever lay ahead. She grabbed Maddy's hand.

"Come on," she said. "There's only one way to find out!"

They ran along the passageways, guided by Gemma's speck of light on the map, until they arrived at the entrance to the burial chamber. There they stopped, horrified by what they saw.

41

Gemma was standing, unable to move, as if held by some invisible force. Towering over her were the gruesome, ghostly forms of two enormous dragons, their jaws drawn back in triumphant leers!

Sesame gasped. The dragon spectres were about to strike Gemma! She *had* to do something . . .

Sesame SPRANG – putting herself between Gemma and the monstrous reptiles. Although she was completely unaware of it, Sesame's aura had a devastating effect on the dragons. She watched in stunned amazement as the grisly creatures recoiled, writhing in agony, their hollow eyes glowing like burning coals. At the same time, their wretched curse over Gemma was broken.

"Sesame!" cried Gemma, suddenly able to speak again. "Don't let them get you!"

The spectres were furious and their deafening roars shook the pillars of the chamber. Sesame shielded her face from the full blast of their fiery breath, as they roared:

I am Smoulder, I am Fume,
You dare disturb our ancient tomb!
Be gone Outworlder, leave us be,
We curse the name of
SESAME!

There was an ear-splitting

BOOM

followed by brilliant flashes of light, crackling and fizzing like fireworks. The girls felt the floor shake.

"Look!" yelled Maddy. "The roof is falling in! Run for it. Now!"

43

And they did. The three girls leaped from the burial chamber, as huge blocks of stone came crashing down. When the dust eventually settled and they dared look back, they could see no sign of the dragons, or the treasure – not even a single coin. Everything was buried under a heap of rubble.

For a moment, the girls stood in the dusty passageway, holding each other.

"Phew!" said Sesame. "I can't believe we got away from those ghastly . . . dragon ghosts."

"Yeah. They were scary!" said Maddy.

"I'm sorry," said Gemma. "It's all my fault! But when I fell down the shaft, something weird happened. I heard voices—"

Sesame suddenly remembered Liz, who was waiting for them at the foot of the shaft.

"Tell us later," she said. "We must get back to Liz.

She'll be wondering where we are!"

"Her light on the map will help us," said Maddy. "Let's have a look."

But when Sesame went to fish the map out of her pocket, she discovered it wasn't there.

"Oh, no! I must have dropped it in the burial chamber. There's no way we'll find it now."

"Well, we'll just have to manage without it," said Gemma. "I got us into this mess, so I'll get us out. Follow me!"

Burial Chamber Maze

Can you help Gemma, Sesame and Maddy find their way back along the maze of passages, to where Liz is waiting for them?

Eight

After watching Sesame and Maddy disappear down the dark passageway, Liz settled herself to wait for them. Her only comfort was the sunlight, streaming down from above and bathing her in a pool of light.

"I'd much rather *read* about secret treasure than go looking for it," she said to herself. She regretted her decision to go with Gemma. "Anyway I bet there's nothing here—"

Her attention was caught by something lying at the foot of the shaft. It was a roll of parchment, tied with a silver ribbon.

"What's this?" she said, picking it up and untying the bow. Carefully she unrolled the scroll and read what was written there:

I, Silvesta, Silversmith of Karisma, on this eighth day in the mede of Arez, this being the fiftieth year of The Gloom, bear witness to the events I have described here.

In the years known as The Gloom, there lived two monstrous dragons called Smoulder and Fume, who were brothers. For fifty years they held the good people of Karisma to ransom. Whether folk were rich or poor, they were forced to give up their silver and gold. Anyone resisting the demands of these greedy brothers paid a terrible price — their homes and crops were destroyed by the monsters' fiery breath, and in this way Smoulder and Fume each acquired vast hoards of treasure.

But in the fiftieth year of this sad time, when treasures were scarce to find, Smoulder and Fume grew envious of one another's ill-gotten gains, and each thought the other had more than his fair share.

One day they quarrelled over a handful of flukes* – just seven small coins. The quarrel turned into a fight, and the fight became a fierce battle! For seven days and seven nights the dragons grappled, clawed, clashed, brawled and blasted each other with red-hot flames, which scorched the land for as far as the eye could see.

On the seventh day of this dreadful contest, when both were weak and near to death, the selfish, heartless dragons made a pact. With their dying breath they cursed anyone who might come after them and disturb their bones to steal their treasure.

"If gold you seek, the price is high;
Your life, for ours – prepare to DIE!"

* *

*Fluke – a small gold coin (Karisman old money) in use before the existence of the Silver Pool

And with these words, they died – and so too ended the fifty years of misery in Karisma known as The Gloom.

Now Smoulder and Fume had a sister called Agapogo, who had nothing to do with her brothers' wicked ways. She was a feisty dragon and cared nothing for her brothers' dying curse. Besides, she knew full well that one dragon may not curse another – there is honour, even among dragons! So Agapogo took it upon herself to return all the stolen treasures to the people of Karisma, and invited them to reclaim their possessions. A few dared risk the dragons' curse, but most Karismans thought it unlucky to possess anything Smoulder and Fume had touched.

So I, Silvesta the Silversmith, having charge over all precious metals, ordered the unclaimed treasure to be buried deep inside this burial mound in a secret chamber, and the remains of Smoulder and Fume be placed there too.

In recognition of Agapogo's gesture of goodwill, our king, Umbriel, gave her a fine collection of silver ornaments. He knew how much Agapogo loved silver! I, myself, fashioned a beautiful silver goblet, which became Agapogo's most treasured possession. As I write, she guards her very own hoard of silver in a cave on Mount Fortuna and, apart from some occasional roars, I'm happy to say she doesn't bother anyone.

As for those seven flukes the dragons fought over? I threw them into the air and where they fell, seven standing stones appeared, which I called The Coins. And on the first stone I carved these words, as a warning to anyone foolish enough to disturb the dragons and their cursed gold!

1

IN A CIRCLE, SEVEN STONES,
GUARDIANS OF OLD DRAGON BONES.
CURSED TREASURE LIES BELOW,
WHERE ONLY FOOLISH FOLK DARE GO!

Then I hid the scroll in this place for safekeeping and whosoever shall find it, may know that this is a true record.

Silvesta the Silversmith

Liz had just finished reading, when Gemma appeared, followed by Sesame and Maddy.

"Oh, Liz," said Gemma. "I've never been so frightened in all my life! It was terrible. There were these two dragons—"

"—Smoulder and Fume," said Liz, waving the scroll. "I found this. It's all about them. You were SO lucky to get out. I think they put you under a curse!"

They scrambled up the shaft and out into the warm sunshine. After the cold, dark, foul-smelling tomb, it was a relief to be in the fresh air. Liz listened in awe, while the others told her about their horrifying ordeal in the burial chamber. Then she showed them the ancient scroll.

"Fantastic, Liz!" said Sesame, after she'd read it. "It's a brill find. Agapogo's silver has been a mystery, up till now. This explains everything!"

Liz beamed. She was pleased to have done *something* useful, while the others were facing such danger.

"Pogo will want to see this," she said. "He'll love reading about his ancestor."

"Okay," said Sesame. "But he can't keep it. He *must* give it to Queen Charm. It's an important part of Karisman history. "

"Good thinking," said Gemma. "And talking of Pogo, isn't time we were getting back? The dragon said we must return by the Seventh Shadow, whenever *that* is. We still haven't a clue what it means."

"And we still haven't found a charm!" said Sesame.

Nine

Sesame looked at the sun lowering in the sky, and guessed they didn't have much time left before the gate closed.

"We *can't* go until we've found a charm," she said. "Maddy and I were at the seventh stone when you came for us, Liz. Come on. Let's all look there."

They retraced their steps to The Coins. The standing stones cast long shadows in the late afternoon sun, and as Maddy stood at the foot of the seventh stone, something twigged.

"Look," she said. "Its shadow is pointing to the gate. *This* is the Seventh Shadow! We must return before it reaches Pogo."

"You're right," said Gemma.

"It's getting longer," said Liz. "We won't have much time to look for the charm."

"I'm *sure* we'll find the coin here somewhere," said Sesame. She looked very determined. "Sesame Brown will track it down! Please, keep looking."

So the girls crawled around on their hands and knees, parting clumps of grass and looking

55

under stones, until Gemma suddenly gave a squeal of delight.

"Here!" she cried. "I've found it. I've *found* it!"

The sun had struck the base of the stone and there, caught in a crack and glinting in the sunlight, was the coin charm. Gemma stooped to pick it up and held it in the palm of her hand. The others crowded round to admire the tiny silver coin, which bore the head of Queen Charm. It glistened with a light of its own.

"Oh," said Sesame. "How lovely!"

"Well done, Gemma," said Maddy.

"Totally brill!" said Liz.

Gemma heaved a sigh of relief and hoped it would make up for her quarrel with Sesame.

"This is the *best* treasure!" she said, handing the coin to her for safekeeping. And Sesame gave her a hug.

Meanwhile, the Charmseekers were being watched! Hidden behind the standing stones were Dork and his men, and hiding from them was Morbrecia.

When Dork saw Gemma hand the charm to Sesame, it was his cue for action. He leaped out, shouting:

"Sesame Brown! Stop in the name of Queen Charm. Once more I find you in possession of Her Majesty's property. Hand it over. You're under arrest!"

The girls gawped at him.

"Oh, not you again," muttered Maddy, under her breath.

"What *is* his problem?" murmured Gemma.

"NO WAY!" said Sesame, clasping the charm firmly in her fist. "I can't believe you're doing this. We're Charmseekers! Can't you see we're trying to help?"

Liz tugged at her sleeve. Out of the corner of her

eye she'd caught sight of several soldiers advancing towards them. Then Sesame saw them too, and someone else – the familiar figure of Morbrecia was lurking in the shadows. Sesame reckoned it was some kind of trap and she knew they had to act *fast*!

"Come on," she hissed to the others. "RUN!"

So the Charmseekers ran flat out, ahead of the lengthening Seventh Shadow. Sesame's quick reaction took Morbrecia completely by surprise. "Blatz!" * she cursed. "Sesame mustn't get away with another charm."

And she pelted after Dork and his men, now chasing the Charmseekers in full cry . . .

✶ ✶
✶ ✶

Pogo had been waiting for the Charmseekers to return. As the Seventh Shadow crept ever closer to his gate, he was afraid they wouldn't make it. So it was a relief when, at last, he saw them racing towards him. But why were Dork and his soldiers pursuing them? And what was Princess Morbrecia doing? The gatekeeper was confused. Absent-mindedly, he swished his long, spiky tail from side to side. *SWISH. SWISH.* Tail swishing had become a habit, whenever Pogo tried to work things out.

* *
✶ **Blatz** – a really angry exclamation

SWISH, SWISH, SWISH!

"What's going on?" he said. "Why is everyone chasing the Charmseekers?"

SWISH!

"Hurry!" he shouted, when Sesame and the others were in earshot.

"We're coming!" yelled Sesame.

After that everything happened at once. Pogo flicked his tail and swept Dork and his men off their feet. The soldiers went flying in all directions!

Morbrecia ducked and plunged at Sesame; she saw she was wearing her locket, so she made a grab for it. But Maddy saw what Morbrecia was up to and pulled her hair, just as Gemma stuck out her foot and tripped the princess up.

"Magworts!" *screamed the furious Morbrecia, now lying flat on her back. She looked up in time to see Dork and his men staggering to their feet. "Doofers!"** she yelled. "Get after them!"

By now, Liz had reached the gate and was thrusting the parchment at Pogo.

"Here," she panted. "Take this. Give it to Queen Charm!"

And with one last effort, all four Charmseekers fell through the gate and into a cloud of mist and stars . . .

* *
* **Magwort** – probably the worst name you could call anyone! General term for a fool
** **Doofer** – idiot of the first order. Brainless

60

Dork was furious with Pogo.

"It's all your fault!" he shouted. "If it hadn't been for your stupid tail, we'd have caught Sesame and her gang of robbers. You should have stopped them."

Pogo looked bemused.

"There must be some mistake," he said. "They're Charmseekers. We gatekeepers have been told by Her Majesty to give them every assistance."

"Well, *I'm* under orders from Her Majesty to arrest them!" said Dork. "They're thieves and you've just helped them to escape. Her Maj will not be pleased, I can tell you."

"Yes, she will," said Pogo brightly. "Give her this." He fished the scroll from under his wing. "Historic document. It contains some very important information about Agapogo. *My* ancestor! I guarantee Queen Charm will be *very* pleased when she reads it."

"Hm," said Dork. "Well, I suppose it's better than nothing."

And he marched off to the palace.

Morbrecia meanwhile had taken the opportunity to slip away to her castle; every step of the way she cursed Sesame for thwarting her yet again.

"I'll be ready next time," she vowed. "Then Sesame Brown had better watch out!"

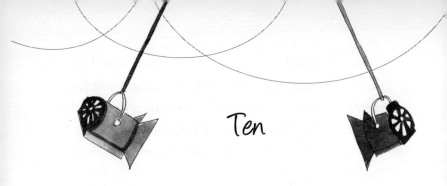

Ten

The girls landed back on the set of *Tomb Robbers*. Seconds later, Samira returned from taking Jason Flook to the photo shoot.

"Hope you weren't bored while I was away," she said.

The four girls exchanged knowing glances. If only Samira knew! Sesame thought their adventure would make a fantastic film but, of course, they couldn't tell anyone about it – yet. She smiled at Samira, as she reached into her pocket to finger the precious little coin charm, and said:

"No. We've had a great time."

"Yeah, loads to see," said Maddy truthfully.

"And do," added Gemma.

"Mm, loads," agreed Liz, wiping silvery mist from her glasses.

"Fab!" said Samira. She turned to Sesame. "Your dad wants to take a picture of you all with Jason and the cast. Follow me, girls!"

So they trooped after Samira to a real standing stone, where Jason and his co-stars were posing for pictures. At the end of the session, Nic lined everyone up for a final shot. I must be dreaming, thought Sesame, as she stood next to Jason.

"SMILE!" said Nic.

And Sesame smiled all the way home.

Later that evening, when Sesame was getting ready for bed, she thought about some of the extraordinary things that happened that day. She looked at the photograph her dad had taken, earlier.

"Look," she told her teddy, Alfie. "There's me with top celeb, Jason Flook!"

But feelings of happiness were mingled with sadness, when her thoughts turned to Karisma. The special jewellery box lay open on her beside table; Sesame was proud to have found eight of the thirteen lost charms and to have put them here for safekeeping, with Queen Charm's bracelet. She couldn't resist taking them out now and admiring them, one by one: the heart with its tiny keyhole; the horseshoe, shell and cat; the delicate little butterfly she'd found in a spider web; the lantern and the snowflake. And now the charming silver coin with its image of the queen . . .

As Sesame replaced the charms in the box and closed the lid, thoughts about Queen Charm whirled inside her head. She felt puzzled and upset.

"Why has the queen turned against me?" she said. "Charm sent Dork to arrest me. She thinks I'm *stealing* her charms! But she must know that's SO not true. It's not fair! I'm doing my best to help her. And I've still five more charms to find—"

Alfie slid sideways off the pillow, so Sesame propped him up again. She unclasped her necklace, and suddenly a vision of Morbrecia flashed in front of her. Sesame remembered how she'd seen the princess lurking near The Coins, and how she'd tried to snatch her locket.

"I wish I could tell Charm about her sister!" she told Alfie. "*She's* the one who ought to be under arrest. Morbrecia is after the charms and she tried to take my locket. Zorgan wants them too. I bet they're working together. Oh, Alfie, it's all *so* confusing!"

For the next few moments, Sesame held her necklace in the palm of her hand. It was very special to her, but why were Zorgan and Morbrecia so keen to have it? The necklace felt warm and tingly to her touch. How weird, she thought. It's as though someone has been listening to what I've been saying! She opened the locket and there were the pictures of her mum, Poppy, and her dad, smiling back at her. Seeing them made her feel much better.

Carefully, she placed the necklace beside her bed and switched off the light. Somehow, she thought, as she snuggled under her duvet, things would work out okay. One day. Until then, she couldn't wait to go back to Karisma to find the missing charms!

Eleven

It was nearly Moonrise and the queen's birthday celebrations were about to begin. Charm had arranged a modest party – not too grand – to which she had invited one hundred important officials and special friends. Ozina was helping Charm with her dress – a shimmering turquoise and emerald gown, covered with sequins.

"Karisma is going through difficult times," said Charm, placing a filigree silver coronet on her head. "Until my charm bracelet has been found, things are unlikely to get better. Which reminds me, I still have the dreadful headache I had this morning!"

"Oh dear, Your Majesty," said Ozina, and tried to think of something to cheer her up. It didn't take long. "Cook's made you a lovely birthday cake!"

Charm smiled.

"Well," she said, "I shall save a piece for you."

The Silversmith was among the first guests to arrive. She stepped out of her horse-drawn carriage in front of the palace gates and gave a little gasp of surprise.

The strange purple cloud that had appeared in her vision, was hanging over the palace. I wonder what it means? she thought, as she hurried inside.

Crossing the elegant ballroom, hung with sparkling chandeliers, she greeted Charm with a curtsey.

"Happy Birthday, Your Majesty," she said. But the Silversmith was dismayed to see her friend looking agitated and concerned, and knew at once something was wrong.

"I must talk to you about Sesame Brown," said Charm, keeping her voice low, and took the Silversmith aside. "I'm convinced your Seeker is a thief! I've ordered Dork to arrest her. There's no mistake this time."

The Silversmith was horrified.

"Oh, but you *are* mistaken," she ventured. "When did this start?"

"Er, this morning I think," said Charm vaguely. Her headache was getting worse. "I was opening my birthday cards after breakfast. Someone sent me some flowers . . . my head started to ache and—"

"What flowers?" enquired the Silversmith suspiciously.

"Those," said Charm. She pointed to the bouquet of dark purple blooms, with their powerful perfume.

The Silversmith caught sight of the card that came with them, and immediately her mystic powers picked up bad vibrations from the handwriting:

To Her Majesty,
Happy Birthday!
from a well-wisher
x x

"Those flowers aren't from a *well-wisher*," said the Silversmith angrily. "They're from ZORGAN!"

Without another word, she grabbed the flowers and flung them out of a window. This simple act had an amazing effect on Charm's headache *and* the purple cloud. They instantly disappeared! Charm looked relieved and confused at the same time.

"Zorgan put you under some sort of doubting spell," explained the Silversmith. "No wonder you thought badly of Sesame."

"Poor Sesame!" cried Charm. "That balam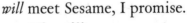 magician tricked me. I wish I could tell Sesame how sorry I am."

"Rashee"** said the Silversmith soothingly, and gave Charm her bouquet of poppies. "One day you *will* meet Sesame, I promise. There'll come a time when we can explain everything to her. Until then, I know she'll go on looking for your charms."

---

*Balam – cursed or damned
**Rashee – hush; be still. A word of reassurance

Just then a red-faced, flustered-looking Dork arrived.

"Ahem. Er . . . I regret to inform Your Majesty that I failed to . . . that is . . . I was unable to arrest Sesame Brown because I, er . . . unfortunately tripped over the gatekeeper's tail—"

"Wonderful!" exclaimed Charm, clapping her hands with joy. "Simply wonderful. Sesame Brown is NOT a thief. I was under some . . . misapprehension. Here, Officer Dork. Have a piece of birthday cake!"

Dork rolled his eyes. He was completely baffled. Girls, he thought. They can never make their minds up! But, of course, he said nothing of the sort to the queen, and handed her the scroll, which Pogo the gatekeeper, had given him.

Charm read it with the Silversmith.

"This is a fascinating part of our history," said Charm, her eyes shining with delight. "Thanks to Sesame and her friends, Agapogo's magical silver is no longer a mystery. Three cheers for the Charmseekers!"

Twelve

The Silversmith arrives in her workshop and the first thing she sees are the thirteen magic candles.

"Ah!" she sighs. "Another candle has gone out. It is the silver coin." It is with Sesame, together with the seven charms she has already found. Eight charms safe in her Seeker's care.

"Good," she murmurs. "Thank you, Charmseekers! You have conquered many dangers to find these precious charms, although I fear there are many more challenges to overcome. Have courage to go on with your quest, Sesame!"

Five magic candles glow and each of them will burn until its lost charm is found – no matter how long it takes.

She crosses to the window and looks out into the starry heavens, reflecting on the strange happenings of the day. So, Zorgan *almost* succeeded in turning Charm against Sesame. This was a powerful spell and cunningly planned. Who knows what might have happened if she had not attended Charm's party tonight! And no doubt the wretched magician has more tricks up his sleeve. Her Seeker must beware . . .

What's this? A shooting star! A heavenly beacon of light, streaks across the sky. To where? All the way to Sesame's world? But that is another story. It must be told another day!